FOR Carmine Agnone, Stefano Barone & Timothy Block

—R.A.

FAMILIUS

Published by Familius LLC, www.familius.com

Familius books are available at special discounts for bulk purchases for sales promotions, family
or corporate use. Special editions, including personalized covers, excerpts of existing books,
or books with corporate logos, can be created in large quantities for special needs. For more
information, contact Premium Sales at 559-876-2170 or email specialmarkets@familius.com.

Library of Congress Catalog-in-Publication Data

2014956435

ISBN 9781939629760

Cover and book design by David Miles

10 9 8 7 6 5 4 3 2

First Edition

Printed in China

RINO ALAIMO'S

THE

BOY

WHO LOVED THE

MOON

any years ago, one night in June, the lights of the city went out, one by one, until only a single light illuminated the sky.

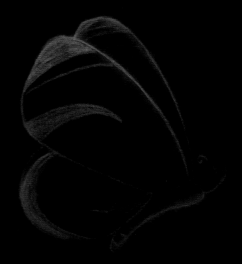

It was the Moon, shining with a radiant glow.
Casting her light through an open window,
she captured the heart of a lonely boy.

Determined to win her affection, the boy endured a long and arduous journey upward to offer the Moon a beautiful rose.

But the Moon, unimpressed with
his gift, gently rejected the boy.

The boy refused to give up. He embarked on a long voyage across the turbulent seas, looking for a worthy gift that could win the heart of the Moon.

For he had overheard whispers that somewhere, deep in the ocean depths, was the most exquisite of pearls.

With the pearl clasped in his hands, the boy rose up to the surface and beyond, up to the blanket of stars to offer the Moon his new gift.

But once again, she declined.

He did not falter. With a broken heart, the boy drew his sword and faced the ferocious dragon of the forest. With one quick swipe, he cut out the dragon's diamond eye.

But the Moon did not care for riches,

and once again, she refused.

Broken and defeated, the boy found himself before an old, ruined house.

The shadow of an old man appeared at the window. He told the boy that there had been others who had tried to win the Moon's love with all the most lavish gifts of the world. But they had failed.

He warned the boy to stop trying. Otherwise,
she would transform him forever.

Hearing this, anyone else would have given up.
But not the boy. In the solitude of his thoughts,
he devised a plan.

He tied the Moon with a long piece of string and held her in place. And as the Sun slowly rose over the dark horizon, the boy finally offered the Moon something she had never seen before . . .

He gave her the beauty
of the colors of the day.

And today, if you look up at the Moon on a dark, magical night in June, you just might see that she's not alone.

For finally, the boy had won the love of the Moon.